THE GREAT COOKIE THIEF

SESAME STREET ®
CTW

BY EMILY PERL KINGSLEY

from an original idea by
Emily Perl Kingsley, Norman Stiles, and Dan Wilcox

ILLUSTRATED BY MICHAEL J. SMOLLIN

FEATURING JIM HENSON'S SESAME STREET MUPPETS

A SESAME STREET/A GOLDEN BOOK

Published by Western Publishing Company, Inc. in cooperation with
Children's Television Workshop. Copyright © 1977 Children's Televi-
sion Workshop. Muppet characters © 1977 Muppets, Inc. All rights
reserved. Printed in the U.S.A. No part of this book may be reproduced
or copied in any form without written permission from the publisher.
Cookie Monster is a trademark of Muppets, Inc. Sesame Street® and
the Sesame Street sign are trademarks and service marks of Children's
Television Workshop. GOLDEN®, GOLDEN® & DESIGN, A GOLDEN
SHAPE BOOK® AND A GOLDEN BOOK® are trademarks of Western
Publishing Company, Inc. ISBN 0-307-58012 ISBN 0-307-68877-1 (lib.
bdg.)

E F G H I J

WANTED

THE GREAT COOKIE THIEF